Chip Chipmunk

Dave and Pat Sargent are longtime residents of Prairie Grove, Arkansas. Dave, a fourth-generation dairy farmer, began writing in early December 1990, and Pat, a former teacher, began writing shortly after. They enjoy the outdoors and have a real love for animals.

Chip Chipmunk

By

Dave and Pat Sargent

Illustrated by
Jeane Huff

Ozark Publishing, Inc.
P.O. Box 228
Prairie Grove, AR 72753

Library of Congress cataloging-in-publication data

Sargent, Dave, 1941—
   Chip Chipmunk / by Dave and Pat Sargent ;
illustrated by Jeane Huff.
   p. cm.
   Summary: Because Chip Chipmunk is a tattletale,
his mother, brothers, and sisters decide to teach him a
lesson which will help him change his behavior.
   ISBN 1-56763-366-8 (cb). — ISBN 1-56763-367-
6 (pb)
   [1. Chipmunks—Fiction.   2. Talebearing—
Fiction. 3. Behavior—Fiction.]   I. Sargent, Pat,
1936—   .
   II. Huff, Jeane, 1946—   ill.   III. Title.
PZ7.S2465Ch   1998   97-27194
[E]—dc21   CIP
                                         AC

Printed in the United States of America

Inspired by

our sitting in the woods near streams, watching chipmunks play. Their continuous chatter reminds us of kids tattling on each other.

Dedicated to

all students who have been called "tattletales." You would have more friends if you stopped tattling on others.

Foreword

Chip Chipmunk is a tattletale. No one wants to play with him. Little Chip's mama and brothers and sisters teach him a lesson with help from Barney the Bear Killer and Sammy Skunk.

Contents

Chip Chipmunk

If you would like to have the authors of the Animal Pride Series visit your school, free of charge, call 1-800-321-5671 or 1-800-960-3876.

One

Tattletale Chip

Chip lived in a burrow. He was three months old and four inches long. He had light-colored stripes on his face, back, and sides. The stripes were bordered by black. The rest of his back, legs, and tail were reddish-brown. His underside was light gray. All his brothers and sisters looked the same; that is, all except for his sister Candy. Her underside was not light gray like the others. Candy's underside was pure white.

All summer and fall, Chip and his brothers and sisters were out scampering along on their long hind legs searching for seeds and nuts to store in their burrow. Even though they would sleep through much of the winter, they might awaken on warm winter days and be hungry.

Chip's favorite thing to do was to tattle on his sister Candy. He tattled on his six other brothers and sisters, but he seemed to pick on Candy. Every time she did the least little thing she wasn't supposed to do, Chip tattled on her. Even if it wasn't really wrong, Chip told his mama anyhow. He was always trying to take care of Candy's business and everyone else's he knew, too. There was no doubt about it, Chip was a little ole tattletale.

"Oh, Chip!" Mama Chipmunk called. "We're going out to gather more seeds and nuts to store for the winter. Come with us. We can use your help."

Chip was busy eating. He was holding a piece of food in his small, slender front feet and nibbling at it with his sharp front teeth. He didn't hear his mama calling.

Mama Chipmunk scampered into the food storage area. There sat Chip, eating away. "Chip! What do you think you are doing? As of last week, this food storage area is off limits until winter. Come with us. We can find plenty of seeds and nuts outside the burrow." Mama nudged Chip with her nose, pushing him toward the tunnel that led outside.

Chip was only four inches long, tail and all. So, a big nudge from his mama really sent him scooting.

As Chip ran through the tunnel, he yelled over his shoulder, "Candy told me it would be okay for me to eat out of the food storage area, Mama. She did! She told me to. It's her fault!"

Mama Chipmunk knew that Chip was a little tattletale. She knew Candy, too, and she knew that Candy would not do such a thing. Candy was a smart little girl. She knew better than to get into the winter food supply.

Mama Chipmunk realized that they must teach Chip a lesson. He needed to learn that being a tattletale was not a good thing.

That evening, after they had stashed their freshly gathered nuts and seeds, Mama Chipmunk called all the little chipmunks together—all except Chip. She didn't tell Chip they were having a meeting, because the special meeting was about Chip.

At the meeting, Chip's brothers and sisters and Mama Chipmunk voiced their ideas about how to stop Chip from tattling.

No matter which idea they tried, nothing worked. They knew they must think of a foolproof way.

Candy said, "Let's get cousin Suzie Q to help. She likes Chip." But then she said, "Bad idea, huh? Suzie Q can't help anyone. Suzie Q would be too busy criticizing."

Chip's brother Chad spoke up. With a gleam in his eye, he said, "All of you know Sammy Skunk. What if we get ole Sammy to agree to spray Chip every time he tattles on one of us?"

All the little chipmunks got excited. They could just see it now. Not only would Chip learn a good lesson, but it would be great fun, too. Just imagine it! Chip the tattletale running in, yelling, "I got sprayed by a skunk!" Boy! They couldn't wait to find Sammy Skunk and ask for his help.

Two

Sammy Helps Out

Later that day, the chipmunks heard a big commotion. It was a coonhound baying. Ole Barney must have been hot on the trail of something. Barney didn't bay just for the sake of baying. He bayed when he was doing some serious hunting. They hurried to the clearing so they could get a better view of whatever was out there causing all the trouble.

Down through the field came Sammy Skunk. And right behind him, in hot pursuit, was Barney.

They figured that Sammy must have done something really bad, like spraying some innocent little animal, just for the fun of it. Barney was probably trying to catch Sammy so he could teach him a lesson.

Sammy must have crawled into a hollow log or something, because fifteen minutes later, ole Barney came back by on his way home. Since Barney hadn't been sprayed, Mama Chipmunk and the young chipmunks figured he hadn't caught Sammy. They knew that if Barney had caught ole Sammy, there would have been a fight, and Barney would have been sprayed, no doubt about it.

"Chad, do you want to find Sammy Skunk and see if he's willing to help?" Mama Chipmunk asked. "I don't want to see little Chip get sprayed, but if it will help . . ."

Chad jumped at the chance. He flew across the field in the direction they had watched Sammy take. It looked as if his feet were not even touching the ground. "I'll find him, Mama," he yelled, as he disappeared in the grass.

Mama Chipmunk said, "Just for good measure, maybe you children should stop playing with Chip until he changes his ways. If no one plays games with him, and you explain to him why you're not playing with him, maybe he will get the message. Do you suppose it would work? What do you think?" They decided to give it a try.

Chad found Sammy asleep in a hollow log. He ran about fifty feet from the log, then started chattering and calling Sammy's name. For all he knew, Sammy might wake up and think ole Barney was about to get him, and he just might let out a heavy mist of that stinky spray.

Sammy opened one eye and looked out. All he could see was a little furry thing. The furry thing looked like his friend Chad. He crawled out of the log and waited for Chad to come closer.

"You're not going to spray me, are you?" Chad asked.

Sammy laughed. "Me spray? Why, I never spray anyone. I'm a nice guy. Everyone knows that."

"Word gets around," Chad said.

Sammy said, "Okay, so I spray sometimes. So what? It's fun!"

Chad asked Sammy for his help in teaching Chip a lesson. And after the two of them decided on a plan, Chad headed toward his burrow, confident that Sammy would not let him down.

That same afternoon, Sammy caught Chip tattling on one of his cousins. He said, "Chip, I'm going to spray you every time you tattle on someone." And with that announcement, he turned, raised his tail, and took aim.

That spraying made Chip stop and think about his bad habit.

Chip was playing outside the next day when he saw a shadow on the ground. Something was soaring overhead. He looked up. He couldn't see a thing with the sun in his eyes. Something swooshed down, and if Chip hadn't run for cover, the hawk

would have gotten him. Boy, that
was close!

Three

Chip Learns a Lesson

Later that day, Chip was going down the trail that ran alongside the creek. He was bored. It was no fun playing by himself. Maybe he would sit on the bank and watch the fish swimming in the creek. He enjoyed doing that.

Just then, Chip heard something coming. He ran underneath some bushes and peeked out. It was Barney the Bear Killer, that ole black and tan coonhound that chased him from time to time.

Barney stopped and sniffed the ground. His nose was going ninety miles an hour. He turned toward the bushes that Chip was hiding under. A half-whine, half-growl came from Barney's throat. It started low, then grew louder and louder as he circled the bushes.

Chip's heart was beating fast. He knew he was all alone because no one would play with him. When the little chipmunks played together and ole Barney got after them, they would all run in different directions. Barney always hesitated that split second, trying to decide which one looked juicier, and they would all escape.

But today, Chip was all alone, because everyone was mad at him for being a tattletale. "So what?" he thought, as he hid under the bushes.

Just then, Barney honed in on Chip. He stretched out his long front leg, flexed his great big ole paw, and extended his nails as far as they would go. He reached under the bushes, made a big swipe, and raked Chip out.

Chip scooted and tumbled free of the bushes. And ole Barney, being the good hunting dog he was, pounced. In a few more seconds, Chip would be no more. No more Chip to tattle on Candy. No more Chip to tattle on his brothers and sisters. No more Chip to tattle on his friends. No more tattletale Chip!

Chip felt Barney's wet mouth close on his head. He felt sharp teeth holding him tight. "No! No! This can't be happening! Not to me!" thought Chip. He pushed with all four feet. "Ouch! You're hurting me!" he yelled. But the sound went right down ole Barney's throat. On the outside of Barney's mouth, not a sound could be heard.

Mama Chipmunk had been looking for Chip. She came along just as Barney raked Chip out from under the bushes, and when she saw Barney's mouth close on her son, her hands flew to her face. "Oh, my," she screamed. "He's eating my baby! I can't see anything but Chip's tail sticking out of that ole hound's mouth. I must do something, fast!"

Mama Chipmunk ran toward Barney, scolding him good! Her sharp little teeth grabbed one of Barney's back legs and held on tight.

Barney looked down. Boy! That little bitty furry thing could sure bite hard! Barney stretched out his leg and shook it hard, but the furry little thing wouldn't let go.

As a matter of fact, when

Barney tried to shake her off, Mama Chipmunk bit down harder. She tasted blood in her mouth. "Good!" she thought. "Maybe now that ole black and tan coonhound will let go of my baby! And if he doesn't, I'm gonna bite his leg off!"

Well, Barney the Bear Killer, being the smart dog that he was, made a fast decision. He figured that the squirming little rodent in his mouth was simply not worth the pain and suffering he was experiencing. So he opened his mouth, and Chip tumbled out.

When Chip hit the ground, Mama Chipmunk grabbed him by the nape of the neck and ran for their burrow. This method of carrying her young worked when Chip was a baby, but now that he was half-grown, he drug the ground! And his nice, soft fur and skin were getting caught on things. Merciful heavens! All this because his little brothers and sisters wouldn't play with him for being such a tattletale!

When Mama Chipmunk and Chip finally reached home, Chip's mama sat him down and asked him a few pointed questions. And when it was all said and done, Chip finally understood that being a tattletale had endangered his life. He decided right then and there that he must change his ways.

Chip searched for his sister Candy. When he found her, he asked for forgiveness for being such a brat. Candy scampered all around him. This was her way of saying, "You're forgiven, brother. Come on, let's play!"

Mama Chipmunk called another special meeting. And this time, Chip was invited. He felt good. With all her young ones gathered round, Mama began.

"All of you know that Chip has always been a little tattletale. Well, Chip has changed his mind. He is not going to tattle anymore. Now, there is one thing I want to make perfectly clear. That one thing is this: Tattling is permissible under one condition. If you know someone is doing something that will cause harm to himself, or herself, or others, you must let it be known. You must either tell me, or you must tell that person's mother or an adult. Is that clear? When your actions can cause someone to get hurt, or killed, then it is not considered tattling. It's okay to tell."

Mama Chipmunk's eyes almost never left Chip's face as she was talking. And Chip's mama could see in his eyes that finally her little Chip understood.

Four

Chipmunk Facts

Chipmunks are small, striped animals. They live in burrows or tunnels in Asia and North America. Chipmunks leave their homes daily to look for food. They hop along on long hind legs, searching for seeds and nuts. They use pouches in their cheeks to carry nuts and seeds to their burrows. They store food in their tunnels.

Chipmunks sleep through much of the winter, but they may awaken on warm winter days and eat some of their food. They eat by holding a piece of food in their small, slender front feet and nibbling at it with their sharp front teeth.

A chipmunk begins its under-ground nest by digging a hole. It carves a tunnel and may make another small opening. The small chipmunk then builds a nesting area by pushing the dirt out. This dirt may plug the first entrance to its nest.

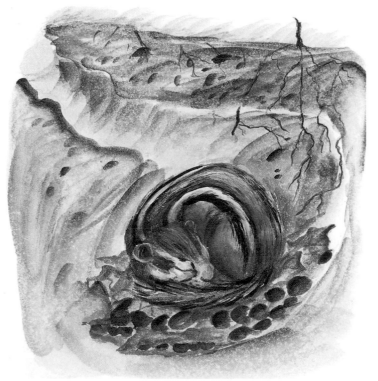

Chipmunks are rodents and are in the same family as woodchucks and squirrels. Chipmunks have short tails and never climb trees. Most American chipmunks are about eight inches long including the tail. They have light-colored stripes on the face, back, and sides. The stripes are bordered by black. The rest of the back, legs, and tail is reddish-brown. The underside of a chipmunk is light gray or white.

Most female chipmunks bear from two to eight young twice a year.

Chipmunks may live two or three years, if they do not become the victims of hawks and flesh-eating animals that prey on them.

Chipmunks are easy to tame. They may learn to take nuts and other food from a person's hand. But even a tame chipmunk may bite or scratch a person and cause a very serious wound.